KEEPING IT TOGETHER

TamRick W

ISBN: 979-8-218-40285-3

CHAPTER 1

WHAT IS THIS?

With many things on her mind Keisha walked into the barber shop, eager to get her nephew's hair cut. The barbershop is a large and spacious area, everything on one level. Five booths on each side. Mirrors and wooden drawers for customers to see their hair when each stylist is finished. "Hello," she said, "my name is Keisha, and my nephew's hair desperately needs cut." The guy smiled and said, "I have two people ahead of you if you don't mind waiting." "How long is the wait?" "Maybe an hour," he answered. "What? I am not going to wait that long! I got things to do." "Okay," he said, looking Keisha right in her eyes. Walking away, Keisha did not know if she would see him again. Not that she cared anyway. The day went on just like a regular day. Keisha could not get her nephew's hair cut that day, but she made sure he looked nice for the occasion and told him to wear a hat. They had fun at Mark's birthday party, Josh's best friend for over three years. Mark had a Ninja party, inviting all his school friends. The amazing feature of the party was the Ninja show that Mark's family included. The adults and children both learned some new karate moves from the famous Ninja, "Naruto." Keisha's nephew Josh lived with her. He was her son, although she had no children. Josh's mother was a big-time drug dealer, and his father was dead. Things were not good for him, and Keisha's sister was too busy on the streets. Keisha's responsibility was to make sure he was all right. The fact that his mother did not have time to take care of him broke Keisha's heart. Angie was always a hustler, thanks to their father; he started her out in the streets early. Everywhere she went he was there, making sure his things were being moved properly. That really wasn't Keisha's thing, so she didn't know how much about it. Their mother was their protector, but Angie wanted to make money, big money. She was deep in it and never wanted to see a loss. Their father taught her everything she knew. Sad to say she did many things that would frighten anyone. All of this started at age ten for her, from beating people to watching horrible crime and selling loads of drugs to people. Honestly, their mother, Sheeba, did not know if she could get her firstborn off the streets. Keisha watched her cry over and over again as Keisha's siblings chose the streets. The money seemed to be lovely, and she had to be real: it was nice being the last child, "the baby." Keisha got everything she wanted from everybody: her father, sister, brother, and uncles. Boy, she was set, especially with her sister—Angie knew how to dress her ass off and brought the finer things for Keisha and herself. Angie ended up dating her oldest brother's close friend. The two became best friends and lovers. Well, that's how Josh came about. His father was a close family friend, and Angie was his everything; the family just knew they would get married. The tragedy happened when they lost him to the streets. He was murdered. The news hit like lighting and left everyone in shock. Angie seemed to have lost everything that mattered to her. Josh was three years old when all this happened, and Keisha has been his mother ever since. Angie supports him financially, but she is not able to manage being a mother to her son, so Keisha stepped up for her and Josh.

⊷═◁ ◁═⊷

"Keisha, you know Josh needs a haircut before school starts," Sheeba says. She pauses and then continues, "Yes, I know you took him last week, but we both know every week is not the same." "Yeah, Ma, I know. Jasmine told me about her barber, Tony. I was interested in taking Josh back there, since the last barber messed up is hairline." "Okay, so go try today; it's Monday." "Yeah, I will, but I'm not ready yet." A couple hours after her mother's warning about Josh's hair, Keisha took the trip back to the barbershop. Upon arrival she noticed the shop was basically empty, with only two people getting their hair cut. Tony was not there, it seemed. Walking in, she asked the receptionist if Tony was there. "Tony? No, he is not here yet, but he'll be here soon, if you don't mind waiting." The only thing she could think at that present moment was that Josh needed his hair cut, so waiting shouldn't be a problem. "Huh, you know what? Here is his number; call and ask him when he will be coming." The receptionist hands her a card. "Okay, thanks." She takes the card and dials the number. "Hello, Tony?" "Uh, yeah," he responds. "This is Keisha. I know you don't know me." "Hi, Keisha, I remember." "Really? You only saw me one time." "Yeah, and how could I forget such a pretty face like yours?" "You could forget, now, we seen each other one time. And that went rather quickly." "You're right, but I have a good memory," Tony reassures her. "Plus, you got a pretty face, as I said before." "Okay, wait, hold fast on the flirting now. My phone call was just to find out if you were coming to the shop." "Sure, I'll be there like in two minutes. Why, are you there? Wait, hold up, you gotta be there. I'll be there soon." "Yeah, I'm here. My nephew needs a haircut, like a real serious one." He laughs at her response. "No problem, I'll be there soon." They both hang up. "Aunt Keisha, I'm hungry," Josh says. "All right, let's go," Keisha responds. "You are so lucky the store is right across the road, because this barber is always busy. He don't waste time, Josh," Keisha complains as they walk across the street to the store. "Hurry up, get what you want. We gotta get back." Keisha rushes Josh. The two walk back to the shop. "Looks like Tony is waiting for us." Keisha looks in the windows of the shop. "We 'bout to be in and out," Keisha expresses. "What? Aunt Keisha, there is no way we could be in and out. Cutting hair takes time," Josh replies. "I know. He better do good, because the last barber messed up your shape." "Agreed, Auntie, 'cause I can't afford another messed up haircut. I'll be mad," Josh adds. "Who you tellin'? Let's see what this man is about," Keisha responds. "Hey, Keisha, nice to see you again," says Tony as they walk in. "Oh yeah, you think so?" "Yeah, the first time I saw you, I thought so, and now it's still the same." "Okay, you're something else." "What type of cut would you like?" "Cut his hair low, and please add a star or zig-zag, something nice." "No problem, will do. Come sit here in the chair," Tony directs Josh. "Do you have a sensitive scalp?" Tony asks. "No, I'm not," Josh responds politely. Keisha sits, waiting impatiently. Man, sitting here waiting is like forever, she thinks, when her phone rings. Keisha expresses loudly, "Thank God my phone rang," then answers, "Hello." Talking to her friend helps the time pass by. "Girl, Lord knows I have no patience when it comes to this. The hardest thing to do is sit and wait for Josh to get his hair cut." Sitting there for forty-five minutes seems like forever to her as time passes by. "Oh, you're finished!" Keisha says to Tony. "Great, I love it! Could you make sure you don't go nowhere? Because you're definitely going to be our new barber." "My pleasure," Tony says. "Could you make sure you keep my number, just in case you need to call me?" "Sure, that's a plus for me. No problem, no problem," Keisha responds.

CHAPTER 2

IT CONTINUES

Walking out of the shop super excited, Keisha looks at Josh and says, "Boy, you look like a superstar. Okay, we are going to buy you an outfit. Then you will look real fly." "Aunt Keisha, I got clothes for days, and you're going to buy another outfit just 'cause my haircut's sweet?" "Yes, boy, and when you start school, you can never look too nice. Now I have to keep up with your haircuts so that you are always looking good." "We know you're great at that, Aunt Keisha." Smiling, Keisha kisses Josh on the forehead. "You're my baby boy; had you since you were three." "Yeah, Auntie, I know. I love you too." Josh smiles. The two go to the store to buy some clothes, and although Keisha was only going to buy one outfit, she ends up buying more. Josh leaves the store with a big smile on his face. The two get in the car and begin driving home. Keisha's phone rings. "Hello," she says. "Hey, what's up, Jas?" "Nothing, Kei did you like Josh's haircut?" Jasmine asks. "Yeah, his haircut is like that, and this time it didn't take long, which was even better...Oh yeah, well, I'm thinking maybe later, but I can't promise, because I got some rearranging to do...Oh well, all right, then. Thanks for calling." Keisha hangs up the phone. Josh and Keisha walk inside the house. "Ma, come look at your young boy. He looks nice, right?" "Oh yes, I love it, Joshy! You know you look great," Sheeba responds. "Josh, go upstairs and relax," Keisha instructs her nephew. "Ma, did you talk to Angie? It would be nice if she'd stop by to say hi to Josh." "Keisha, I told you that Angie is not going to come right now. It's too risky; you know the stuff she's on." "Yeah, but her son misses her, Mom. Sometimes I can't fix that situation. He's not saying it, but I could see it in his eyes, Ma. He needs her!" "Keisha, Angie is not going to come our way right now. Things seem to be getting worse, Kei. You know your sister. If it were good, she would be here. This is not about money; this is about safety. She just wants to keep us safe." "So you're telling me that war has taken place again." "Kei, I didn't want to tell you, but yes. Justin said some guy they trusted ran off with some things, and now they went at him. Well, he got some people he hangs with protecting him. So now Angie is staying away until she feels things are safe." "Ma! I hate this, because who's to tell if things will be safe?" "Kei, you know all we can do at this point is mind our business and take care of Josh. Angie is going to be extra cautious because she lost her lover because of things like this." "So why can't she just leave the shit alone, Ma?" "Baby girl, I asked her to several times. What can we do? Tell me something we can do. I've been trying for years. She has a son, and that still ain't stopping her, so you tell me," Sheeba repeats. She walks off, upset. Keisha picks up her phone to make a call. "Yow, what's up, Kevin?" "Uh, nothing, just concern. You heard from Ang?" "Oh, word, naw, I don't know." "So what now? 'Cause we need to know if where we at is good. Come on, tell me how serious the shit is." "Oh, okay. Let me know if you feel uneasy. Ang is risky, as if people won't look up her history. Things are crazy out here." "The fact y'all lost two guys and money is what gets me. Why can't she just give the business to Justin? Dad even told her to sit down when James died." "Ang just feels like no one else can make decisions like her. Josh miss her? She could put the shit down. We don't want to lose her too." "Yeah, I try to be understanding, but it's much harder when I see my nephew wanting his mom." "All right, yeah well thanks," Keisha says. She hangs up the phone and says out loud, "My sister just doesn't get what this shit does to us." The day goes by fast. Keisha has her sister on her mind. She felt something was not right. She reaches out to her brothers, but it seems like their minds are not on the same idea Keisha has for her sister. She wants the best for Josh.

A month later Josh has started school and is already weeks into it. The time for getting his hair cut approached rather quickly in Keisha's eyes. "Josh, Saturday we will go to the barbershop. I will call Tony and see if we can get the first appointment." "Okay, Aunt Keisha," Josh responds. "Things will get better; I will make sure of that for you." "No prob, Aunt Keisha." "I don't get this no prob thing. Is it your slang or something?" "Naw, it's just an abbreviation for no problem." "I love you. Always keep cool, Josh." "Well, you know how that goes, Auntie." He smiles. "What do you want to eat?" "I think fried chicken with mac and cheese would be good." "Really? Usually you want spaghetti." "Yes, but I thought a change might be nice especially since you give me the choice." "I think that's a lot better than me choosing all the time." "Yeah, I think so too, Auntie, because sometimes you give me way too much vegetables." "Hahaha, you're still getting some sort of vegetable with your food today." Keisha smiles. "So, Josh, how do you like fifth grade?" "It's cool. I have some good friends. My teachers are helpful. I'm happy at school." "Good. I want you to be happy; it's important to feel that way." "Thanks, I'm truly grateful for that, Keisha," Sheeba says, walking into the kitchen. "Well thanks, Ma, it is only true love." "Grandma, do you like to see me happy?" Josh asks. "Of course, baby, of course, but don't forget, when I correct you I'm only teaching you the better things in life. You know I just want you to be the best at whatever you do, even when things don't seem that way. I love you, Joshy, I love you!" "I love y'all; I just wish for my mom sometimes because…" he pauses. "Well, because I miss her and my dad, you know? She is just different, and I don't know why she stays away from me. She don't like me, but other people like me. I'm guessing that's all that matters." "No, Josh, don't say that. Your mother loves you so much. She wanted the best for you," Keisha reassures him. "Well, she has a weird way of showing it." Josh walks away. "See, Ma, this is what gets me, and I understand Ang, but still, she's been lacking. Not coming around is still not safe," Keisha expresses. Immediately Sheeba begins to pray as she felt Keisha's energy of frustration. "Lord, my kids are everywhere, and the one kid that's not in the streets is becoming frustrated. Please, help her with strength," Keisha's mother cries out. "Please, losing her would hurt me. She has taken on the strength for the family. Josh needs her, I need her, and my daughter needs her. Lord, please give her the wisdom she needs to raise Josh, and let his mother be more involved, because she has given up. Lord, the boy needs his mother." Sheeba sits and cries as she feels the pain running through her heart.

CHAPTER 3

BY SURPRISE

A couple of days later, Keisha takes Josh to get his hair cut. "Hey, Josh, let's go. Tony is on his way to the shop, and I'm trying to get there before any other people, you know." "Yeah, I guess, Auntie." Josh runs down the stairs. "I'm ready now!" "Cool, let's go." The two hop in the car and leave. Driving to the shop, Keisha ask Josh what he wants for his birthday. He hesitates and then says, "I don't know. What do you think I should get?" "Excuse me, boy," Keisha replies. "You cannot be asking me that. It's your birthday, not mine, and I would like to know what you want ahead of time so you can have it, Josh." "Huh. Well, of course I want a video game. Then maybe a party, because we ain't had a party since I was seven." "Okay, sounds good to me. I think I could get a party together in three weeks. Let me know what three kinds of food you really want there." "All right, that's what's up. Auntie, you know I love spaghetti, and then fried chicken sounds like a plus as well." "All right, that's two. I guess everything else is left up to me." "Yes, Auntie, yes, we good on the good note," Josh says with excitement. "So, what I'll do is get invitations to you with our menu in a week." "Yes, I'm super happy. I got a lot of friends," Josh expresses. "Okay, we are here. Let's see how it looks in this place." Keisha exhales. "Barbershop trips be the worst, but Tony can cut hair, so I guess it's worth the wait. Oh, lucky, on a Saturday nobody is here yet, Josh." Keisha walks up to the counter. "Good morning, is Tony here?" "Yeah, he'll be out soon." "Okay, thanks," Keisha responds. Tony walks out from the back room. "What's up? Nice to see you." "Well thanks, nice to see you too. Could you do you on Josh's head?" Keisha asks. "I got you, Keisha," Tony replies. She smiles and walks away, thinking, He is so handsome, man. Tall, slim, and dark skin—my type all the way. She sits in the chair and waits for Tony to finish cutting Josh's hair. "Keisha, could we talk after this? I need to ask you something," Tony says as he admire her body. "Oh, that's not a problem," Keisha answers. Her mind begins to run as she thinks about Josh and making his birthday party the best party ever. Taking out her phone, she begins to look up some stuff for the party. Oh, this looks good. I know exactly what theme to use, she says to herself. Keisha screenshots the images she finds of use for the party. Yup, the basketball theme is the best idea. Oh, and people could wear jerseys; that will set the vibes. Keisha begins to smile. "Look at you smiling as soon as I walk over to you," Tony says openly. "Excuse you. I'm thinking about my nephew's party, that's all." "Oh, you having a party?" "Yeah, his birthday is in a few weeks, so I was just think-ing of his theme. I have some great ideas, and I'm sitting here smiling. Now look at you coming over here thinking the smile is about you." "Well, Keisha, that's what I see." "Okay, Tony, what did you want to talk about?" "Could we walk to your car so we can talk?" "Yeah, I guess so, that makes a lot of sense," Keisha responds. They begin walking to her car. "Come on, Josh, get in the car, because Tony and I need to talk." Josh gets in the car. "Ms. Keisha, let me ask you politely: could I take you out and have a nice dinner?" "When are you planning to do this?" "When are you able to?" "I'm not sure, because you know I have

Josh." "Yes, please excuse me for asking, but is it possible you could have someone watch him? Listen, you have my number; call me so we can figure a date maybe." "Okay, let me see what my schedule will be like and confirm with you." "Sounds good. Looking forward to your call." Keisha smiles as she gets in the vehicle. Her thoughts are, Damn he is so fine. Like, he is way too attractive to be in anyone's barbershop. Keisha laughs out loud. "All right, your hair is cut. We could go to a restaurant and enjoy some food." Josh smiles. "Aunt Keisha, you always doing things with me; it never stops. I love yah." "Josh, it's us; that's all we got. Family takes care of family." Taking notes in the back seat, Josh responds, "Man, I'm just trying to get things done now I know we are having a party. You agreed to that today, and you have three weeks." Keisha laughs. "Josh, that's true, but in order to have a great turnout, we must start now. We are here," Keisha says with excitement. "Pizza place it is!" Josh shouts. "I love, love pizza." "We could sit here; Josh, go wash your hands." Two men walk in, looking Keisha straight in the eyes. "Excuse me, do I know you?" she asks. "Naw, you don't know me, but I know your sistah. Tell G we see how she move." "Huh? What are you talkin' about?" Keisha asked, frightened. "Stop playin' like you don't know." "Look, I don't know you, and as far as this G person you're talking 'bout, I'm unsure who you're talking of." "You stop the shit; Malcolm told us where you be at, so we followed you. We been watching you, so like I said, tell G we see how she move. Oh, let her know shit is real. Damn, this your son?" "Yes, that's my son." "Oh, I guess it runs in the family. He looks just like G." "Look here, you should leave. You coming here is pointless, and you will no longer harass me or my son." Keisha stands up and walks toward the cash register. "Yeah, aight, tell G what we said. I'll know if you sent the message." The men walk out of the restaurant. Keisha grabs Josh and kisses him. "Aunt Keisha, why are you shaking?" "Okay, Josh, don't call me Aunt, call me Ma or Mom, okay?" "All right, calm down, calm down.

Please stop shaking." "Well damn, I don't know where to start or even…okay, we will eat and then go home." Keisha orders their food, and while waiting she talks to Josh, trying to remain normal. She feels terrified, and it's hard to hide. Josh is quiet and looks at his aunt as she speaks. He knows something is strange but doesn't want to ask. Keisha tries to distract Josh with questions about his party. Josh finally bursts out with it. "Aunt Keisha, who were those people?" he asks in a concerned manner. "Oh, those were some people from years ago. I told them to let it be. We are okay; we will be okay," Keisha says in a low voice. "It just shook me up a bit, that is all." "Oh, well, okay, you can relax now. They're gone. I seen them drive off." Keisha smiles, trying her best not to cry. "Yeah, they are gone. You're right, Josh. Well, our food is here; let us enjoy." The two ate their food and drank frozen drinks. "One of my favorites," Keisha says as she continues to slurp her drink. "Man," she says later as she pays the bill.

CHAPTER 4

REALITY

"It's time to go, Josh." Keisha can't help but to feel odd as she walks to her vehicle. The car ride home is incredibly quiet. "Josh, when you get in the house, go and take a shower," Keisha instructs him as she pulls into the garage. "All right, Ma," Josh answers as they enter the house. Keisha exhales as she walks in her living room and sits down. "What the heck," she says to herself. "I can't believe Malcolm; I can't believe his ass!" she shouts. "What in the fuck, man!" Keisha is angry. She can't believe her sister's best friend—well, real good friend—would do that. Her phone rings. "Hello," Keisha answers, sounding like the whole world is on her back. "Hey, Jas, I'm so fed up right now. The life given to me I'm grateful for, but the shit around it is not what I want to consider. Girl, two unknown men came into Lamaze and was like, tell G we see her…Girl, yes, and they looked strapped. Of course it was a threat, what else? The only thing to do was play it off…No, they didn't hurt me or Josh…Yes, thank God. He then said, 'Don't play me. We been following you. Malcolm told us how y'all roll.' At that point I couldn't fake it. I ain't said nothing, but still, why Malcom do that?" Keisha begins to cry. "Jas, yes, come over; I do not want to be here, but I gotta make it as normal as possible for Josh…All right, thanks for doing that. I'm gonna call Malcolm, 'cause he is going to answer questions." Keisha hangs up and dials Malcolm's number. The phone rings and rings and rings—no answer. What am I doing? She calls her brother. "Hey, Kevin." Keisha begins to cry. "What, Keisha?" her brother shouts into the phone. "You found out about Malcolm? We tried to keep y'all away from the shit." "No, instead, Malcolm's going around telling people where we live. He told whoever them niggas are all about us. They been watchin' me." Keisha begins to tell the story. "Yes, Kevin, in the pizza place…Yeah, Josh was with me, and they were like, 'Josh look like Angie'…No, no, that was it. They said they see how she is. One was tall with dark skin; the other was chubby with dreads, and yeah, short—like I'm taller than him…No! I'm moving out of all the drama. We manage to keep ourselves out of you all's lifestyle. This is bigger than James, even with James's death… Kevin, no one came to the house." Keisha continues to cry. "We are going to move after Josh's birthday party. I am moving!… Security, what is security when they know where we live?…All right, I will let your dumbass sistah know what they said. Oh, and for Malcolm…What! When?…Oh, this shit is recent? Oh no! Oh no!" Keisha drops the phone and cries. Sheeba walks in the living room. "Kei, what's the matter?" "Nothing. Oh hell, Ma, they killed Malcolm. This war shit is getting serious. Two men approach me at a restaurant, talking about they be watching us." "What?" Sheeba sits down. "Okay, calm down, baby." She rubs Keisha's head. "We know the life they live. We are going to have to separate from them. We have been here for years, but now it's time to reconsider. The people my kids deal with have no heart. We seen it before. We ain't going to stick around to see it again." "Yes Ma, I know. I am sure of that. The only thing is Josh's birthday." Keisha takes a deep breath. "Kei, you could rent somewhere to have Josh's party. I prefer to be there—hell,

I prefer for us all to be there," Sheeba expresses loudly. "Yeah, I get it, Ma. You're right," Keisha agrees. "Ma, to pack and plan is a bit much all at the same time. The next thing is working; you know I am a receptionist at one of the top real estate companies. My work is almost always busy, Ma. It's just complicated to do it all," she complains. "Look, we could find a place and move a few things if we have to, Kei. We can't stay here until Josh's birthday; that is three weeks away from now. A lot could happen in that time frame." "But, Ma," Keisha says. Sheeba interrupts her. "Kei, there is no but. We must do it; this shit could get real nasty as far as I am concerned. Listen, baby girl, we need to be safe for ourselves and Josh." "All right, I will start looking for another place tomorrow." "Great. Check up by City Bay; there are some nice houses over there. We could start out with renting, because buying a house is not going to work right now," Sheeba suggests. "What do you mean, Ma?" Keisha asks. "You know that is a long process. We have to rent a place for now, Kei." "All right, I get it. Just please do not make me do all the work," Keisha says in a calm voice. "You know I'm not going to do that. I will do the packing up of our things while you do a search for places to rent. Oh, and you have to sell this house. I know your father brought it, but we have to sell it." "All right, Ma, just give me some time to process it, and I shall be fine. Well, at least that is what I think," Keisha responds to her mother.

CHAPTER 5

PREPARATION

The next day Keisha begins her search for a new place. She walks into her job, trying to maintain a smile on her face. "Hey, Keisha, how are you feeling?" a coworker asks." "I'm fine. Why do you ask?" "You look out of it." "Really? Just a little tired, that is all." She tries so hard not to cry. It's hard to keep it all in, but once again, she is able to hide her emotions. Sitting in her office, Keisha looks up houses for rent. Well damn, these people ask for a lot. This process is not immediate, either; there are steps to this too. Writing down seven different places, Keisha feels hopeful that she will be successful in moving. Her long-term plan is moving completely out of their current state of Maryland, as going out of state would put them far enough from all the drama. "I will start a new life with my family and get away from all this shit," she says aloud. Tears flow from her eyes down her face. "Right now it does not seem like reality, but I will make it reality," Keisha thinks aloud while driving home. Looking back several times, Keisha checks to make sure no one is following her. While at work, she was able to connect with three out of the seven people about the houses for rent. "When I get home, I will show Sheeba the houses of interest. You know, at times it feels a bit much, but it's all for Josh," Keisha encourages herself. "Hey, Ma," Keisha greets her mother as she enters the house. "Since it's Sunday, many people were available. There are seven houses on my list, but I was able to connect with four out of them." "Go ahead, Kei, you move fast, you know? Baby girl, what is happening now, it is supposed to happen," Sheeba says. "Well, one person will meet with us today at five. Did anyone come here, any unfamiliar faces?" Keisha asks. "No, Kei, no one came here. Josh and I have been cleaning and packing up. Josh wanted to know why we are packing things up," Sheeba informs Keisha. "Well, what did you say, Ma?" "I told him it is time for a change." "That is all you said?" "Yeah, after that he didn't ask nothing else." "Oh well, I must have this talk with him. He already goes through changes in life not having his mother around." Keisha grunts. "Yeah, I know, and that's why I left it just right there," Sheeba expresses. "Yeah, I guess," Keisha responds. "Josh! Josh!" she calls. "Yes, Auntie?" he responds. "Come down here," Keisha shouts. "Hi, Aunt Keisha." Josh hugs her. "Hey, Josh, what is up? How was your day?" Keisha asks. "My day was good. I helped Grandma pack up some things. Why are we moving?" Josh asks in a concerned tone. "We must move because the house needs reconstruction." "What does that mean?" "Oh, it means the house needs to be fixed up." "Well, Aunt Keisha, why didn't you say that?" Josh asks. "Josh, it was not time to say anything until now. Plus, we want to have a party in the new house." "Okay, that sounds good." "Yeah, yeah, Josh, and today we will look at one of the houses. Are you excited?" "Uh, I don't know," Josh answers. "Well, I understand you might not like change, but this change will be all right, okay?" "Yes, Aunt Keisha," Josh responds. "Guess what, Josh, your birthday is going to be sweet. Trust me, okay, baby?" "Yeah." "We have to look at a house on the far north side." "All right, getting ready now." Josh runs up the steps. "Ma, you should do the same, because I'm not going to be late. I need to start ordering stuff for Josh's party, which is going to come up rather quickly." "Kei, I am ready; can't you see that?" Sheeba responds. "Where is this house?" "Oh, it's in Columbia, Maryland." "All right, I guess that's far, though." "Yeah, I know, but they have some nice houses over there." "Kei, I like PG County, honestly; I'd rather stay on this side." "Ma, we need to get as far away as possible, so you ain't got to keep worrying about being safe. We have to move, all right?" "All right, fine. You always make good decisions, so I will trust you," Sheeba admits. "The drive out there is bound to be far and long." "Yeah, Ma, that's why I said get ready. It's about to be four, and it takes us about forty-five minutes to drive out there. Yes, it's a drive, but not that bad. You'll be good," Keisha reassures her mom. "Well, as I said, ready and waiting on you." "Josh, come on, we are leaving," Keisha calls to her nephew. Josh comes down the stairs. "Aunt Keisha, do you think I could get another gift instead of the party?" "Why, Josh, you don't want a party anymore?" "Nah, we don't need to do all that, Aunt Keisha." The three get in the car as Josh continues to speak. "Aunt Keisha, I could wait." "No, we will have a great party, Josh, and you don't need to worry about anything. Talking about that, Ma, I'm thinking to hire Stacy's aunt Shelia's soul food company. She will charge a decent price. I'm thinking spaghetti, fried chicken, mac and cheese, potato salad, BBQ chicken, and french fries. You know, we need a veggie platter and fruit salad. Also, we need some juices, punch, and stuff like that. Yes, we need party flavors, all that. I'm just going to hire people to do the entire party so I'm not stressing," Keisha explains. "Could you call Angie and touch base with her about the drama? She needs to send more money this month. Ten thousand is not going to work; we need double to move and have a party." "Baby girl, you already know I was going to get in touch with her," Sheeba responds. "Sounds good." Keisha smiles as she drives. "You know, I am thinking to get new furniture so everything we have in the house we could give away." "Keisha, you don't need to buy nothing. Move that furniture and keep it." "No, Ma, if we're going to start new, then it doesn't make sense to have old furniture for a new house." "Whatever, Keisha, because you're always going to come up with something new. You know, this is where you remind me of your dad, like serious stuff." "Ma, nothing is wrong with me being like my dad. I think that is the best thing ever, you know. My dad is like that." Keisha laughs. "Anyway, we are here. Where should I park?" "Over there, Kei, says 'visitor parking.' What is the house number?" Sheeba asks, looking around. "The house number is 100127," Keisha responds. "I think it's that house over there." She points to the other side of the road. "Aunt Keisha, this place looks smaller than our house." "Yeah, Josh, but let us go and see what it looks like inside." They get out of the car, and Keisha pulls out her phone. "Hello, yes, this is Ms. Mayer. I'm here…Okay, great." She walks up three steps. "The porch is nice. If we get it, I'll put chairs out here. Oh, it is beautiful on the outside." The door opens and a light-skinned lady greets them. "Hi, you all can come in. So here is the kitchen to your right, and on the left is the dining room. You all can take your pick on where to start." "Let's start with the kitchen. Oh, it has an island, how cute," Keisha compliments. "Oh, it also has a pantry. I love this, Ma, we could even fit a table in here," she says with excitement. "Oh, what is that to your left?" "That is your living room," the realtor says. "The living room is big," Keisha responds. "Yeah, this house is spacious," Sheeba adds. "Oh, and the dining room is con-nected to the living room. I see, it's one big area," Keisha responds. "Yeah, it's nice," Sheeba compliments. "All right, now let's go up the stairs to see the bedrooms." "Huh, wait, where is the backyard?" "Oh, sorry, you did not see the door in the living room area. Yes, you can open it." Keisha opens the door. "Cool, Aunt Keisha, it has a door to another room!" Josh becomes excited. "This is a small storage room, but the sliding door takes you to the backyard, and it has a small patio attached." "Look,

Aunt Keisha, it's a nice space here. Wow, I love it!" Josh exclaims. "You should. We are not finished, Josh, let's go." Sheeba redirects him. The four walk to the front area of the house. "Here are the stairs." "Oh, it's like thirty-five steps to get upstairs," Sheeba complains. "I know, Ma, but look at how the staircase wraps around. It's a long banister, right? We can look down from here." "We could look down from upstairs and see who is coming in the house, like some superstar house," Josh adds. "Excuse me, how many rooms are up here?" Sheeba asks. "There are four rooms: Here is the master bedroom to your right. On your left is a nice size bedroom. The right corner room is not too big, but doable. The left corner room is just a little bigger. It has carpet." "I like it," Keisha replies. "Great! So the last location is the basement. It is big." "Really? Are there any rooms down there?" "Yeah, there are rooms down there. Two bedrooms, not super big," the lady explains. "There is a bathroom, mini kitchen, and living area, as well as a laundry room." "Oh, okay, let me see." "Aunt Keisha, this looks good. Wow my mom could live with us." Keisha and her mother look at each other when Josh expresses his feelings. "Josh, it's nice for real," Keisha comments. "All right, Marie, I will put my application in. How long is the process?" "The process usually takes seven to fourteen days, but if everything is cleared and you are preapproved, it would be the deposit most importantly." "Do you have other applicants?" Keisha asked. "Well, yes, but we are looking for the best applicant." "Okay, well, we will keep in touch," Keisha responds. "All right, bye, nice meeting you." Sheeba shakes Marie's hand. "Let's go, Josh." "Grandma, I am right here with you." "Ma, what do you think about the house?" "I think it's nice, but you know, it's far already, Keisha, but yeah, it's good."

CHAPTER 6

APPROVAL

Keisha looks for houses and puts in applications while waiting for Marie's call. The house is packed up; the only thing left to do is move the large furniture. Driving home from work Tuesday, Keisha makes a phone call. "This is Ms. Mayer. I'm on my way to look at the vacancy…Yes, I am interested; my nephew's party is in two weeks…Yes, the gentleman that picked up earlier said you all have a pavilion in the back as well as a large field and a guesthouse. My nephew will love it too…Yes, I will be there shortly." Keisha drives to the venue, which is ten minutes away from her house. The location for Josh's party seems to be working out, and I was stressing out. Everything is coming together. Keisha exhales. After putting down a deposit for the place, Keisha drives home. Man, I need to call Tony and ask him to cut Josh's hair for his party. Keisha dials his number, and the phone rings a couple of times. "Hello. Tony, it's Keisha. I wanted to know if you could cut Josh's hair for his birthday…Yes, Tony, I know you will do his hair for me; I'm just reserving ahead of time…No, I didn't forget about our date…Yeah, it's been a week and more. To tell you the truth, I have been going through some deep shit." Keisha takes a deep breath. "Well, what is the stuff?" Tony asks. "I'd rather not say; it may scare you or even alarm you." "No, you won't do none of that. I've seen some things," Tony replies. "No, it's okay." Keisha continues to avoid the details of her situation. "All right, so when will we go out? I'm sure you need a break." "Huh, right now I'm in the middle of trying to move somewhere else, so after I move, we could go out…Yeah, I'm sure…Oh, Tony, that is nice. I will call you for sure if I need to talk. Thanks for everything," Keisha says before hanging up the phone. "Home soon to be another home," she speaks aloud. "Hey, Ma and Josh," Keisha greets her little family as she enters the house. "Hi, did the lady call you?" Sheeba asks anxiously. "No, she didn't call. Maybe tomorrow, Mom." "Josh, go upstairs," Sheeba instructs her grandson. "Kei, today some men were watching the house." "Wait, what?" Keisha asked, confused. "Yes, a van parked outside all day." "Wait, Ma, are they still there?" "No, not that I notice, but it could change, you know." "What color van?" Keisha asks. "The van was gray." "Ma, how do you know they were watching us?" "Josh went to take the trash out, and a guy came out of the van. He was asking Josh questions. That's when I told Josh to come in the house." "My gosh, Ma, what in the hell?" Keisha shouted. "Josh! Come here, come now." Keisha's phone rings. Josh comes down the stairs. "Yes, Aunt Keisha?" he answers. "Go sit down. I'll talk to you in a min- ute. Hello, yes, Ms. Mayer speaking. How are you?…Oh yes, yes, I'm glad you have chosen us. I can get the money to you by the end of the week…Yes, we are ready to move in. Thank you so much." Keisha hangs the phone up. Thank you, God, thank you, God; it's only you I could thank. "Josh, hey, baby, the guys earlier today—what did they say?" Keisha asks Josh. "He asked me if Uncle Kevin lived here." "What? And what did you say?" "Nothing. I told him I didn't know anyone by that name." "Good, I'm proud of you. I did not teach you that, Josh, how did you know to say that?" Keisha asks. "Aunt Keisha, if someone is asking about Uncle Kevin, then it's not good." "Huh, what makes you say that, Josh?" "He barely comes home, and all his friends or anyone that knows him knows where he stays at. Remember, Uncle Kevin takes me with him sometimes." "Well, Josh, you're smart. Good job today. You can go back upstairs. Oh no, wait, what did he look like?" "He was fat and short." Keisha looks outside again to make sure she does not see the van. "Okay, Josh, thanks. Go upstairs. Ma, call your son and give him the details Josh just shared. We got the place; we will move Friday. For now, you guys will stay in a hotel until then." Keisha sits on the couch. Man, I don't feel at ease. I need to figure this shit out. Damn, what is the point, really? Like, it don't make no sense. She picks up the phone and calls her friend Stacy. "Hello, Stacy, we're coming over tonight, all right?…Thanks, Stacy. When I get there, we can talk." Keisha hangs up and calls, "Ma!" "Kei, I'm talking to Kevin." "Josh, get your packed bag and let's go." "Where are we going?" "We are going to stay over at Stacy's house. Ma, are you still on the phone?" "Yeah, but go ahead; what you saying?" Sheeba asks. "Get your bag, Ma, we're leaving now. We ain't staying here, because these people are strange and suspicious. I don't trust it." "All right, Kei, that sounds good. Josh, get my bag; everything is already in it. Kei, did you get your stuff?" "Ma, I put it in the trunk just in case of shit like this. Let's go. Man, I can't believe this; it's not even fair." Keisha complains continuously. "Like, I didn't choose this life, so why we gotta be running like we robbed the bank?" Keisha begins to cry. "Come on, Josh. Ma, lock the door. Do you see any strange cars?" "Naw, Auntie, everything looks the same to me," Josh answers calmly. "Keisha, there are no new cars, girl, stop worrying." Sheeba tries to comfort her. "It is easier said than done, Ma. Out of nowhere these problems come. The sad part to it is I have nothing to do with it." "Kei, you are related to the people who do have something to do with it." "Yeah, I know that! Ma, I know that!" Keisha shouts out of frustration. "Well, as long as you know. We will be okay. Let's not get too worried or anxious," Sheeba says. Keisha knocks when they arrive, and the door opens. "Josh, you can go upstairs with Ryan," Stacy says. "Hey, Ma, make yourself welcome," she continues. "Oh, and well, come on, girl, let's talk it over." The two ladies go down the steps into the basement. "Come on, let's sit on the couch. All right, so what's up?" "Girl, it's your beau, Kevin, and his siblings," Keisha complains. Stacy laughs. "Kei, I know the shit is serious, 'cause Kevin told me. People getting shot left to right. Oh, and dying too." "Stacy, I'm gonna need you to get real serious with this." "I am, but guess what, I know what this shit is about, you know." "Oh yeah, has anyone been following you?" "Naw, they not going to follow me. Why should they?" Stacy asks. "You're Kevin's woman, right?" Stacy laughs. "Yeah, but to be completely honest, they want Ang and Justin." "So if that's who they want, why they ask about Kevin?" "Wait, hold up, Keisha. They asked about Kevin?" "Yes, they asked about him." "Woah, I didn't know that." Stacy's tone begins to change. "So what, did they run up in the house?" "No, that's not the case; that's not what they did." "Oh, so what? What, tell me," Stacy asks, panicking. "Josh went to throw the trash out, and the guy approached him, asking if Kevin lived there." "So what did he say?" Stacy asks. "Josh said he don't know anybody named Kevin, and Ma told Josh to come in the house." "That's all?" Stacy asks. "No, Ma said they been watching the house all day." "Man, Keisha, this is crazy. What is your plan? Because if they're looking for Kevin, then they may come here." "You see how you are, Stacy? When you thought they was looking for Ang and Justin, it was no problem. Look, tomorrow take Ma and Josh to the Marriot up the street. Make sure you check them in, okay? I'm going to work, because that's important." "No one has come here, and I hope they don't," Stacy complains. "I gotta call Kevin." "See, Stacy, the bull has become real. I told you it's serious. Did you speak to Ang?" "Yeah, Ang's outta town, and Justin is the one in business." "We spoke to Kevin already; he knows what's up." "Damn, he ain't called me," Stacy replies. "He'll call you, Stacy. Plus, they did not come here. If anything, they may keep going to the house. Oh, and Josh says the van is gray. I need to figure out my safe place. Stacy, they did not come here at all." "No one stopped you?" "No one." Keisha comforts her. "Look, Kevin's information, ID, all that is at the house. Everything he got registered is with that address, so we just need to move from that house, that's it. They know everything about him, and, well, never mind. I just gotta move." The family continues to rest their heads at the Marriott for the week. Friday morning Keisha goes to pick up the keys for the new place. Man, I don't even know what to do. Keisha sits in her vehicle trying to think things through. Oh, I could call Tony. "Hey, Tony, what's up with you? I know it's been a while." "Yeah, it's been a while. You good?" Tony asks. "Yes, I'm okay. How about you?" "Well, I've been working and things like that. Are you calling about our date?" "No, but that will happen." "Oh, is that right?" Tony responds. "Could you help me move?" Keisha asks. "Wow, that sounds like something I'm interested in." Keisha laughs. "The only thing is I'm going to show you where, and my girl Jasmine will be in charge of moving the things. Her brothers will help you. Do you have any friends that could help?" "Yeah, my nephew could help. But you good? 'Cause you sound like you're stressed." "No, I'm good. It's only because I have a lot to do for Josh and his party in two weeks." "Oh, okay, so will I see you?" Tony asks. "Yeah, you'll see me at the new place." "So what, you got a surprise for me at this new place?" "No, I said we will go out. I just got this shit to take care of first," Keisha reassures him. "All right, Keisha, I'll be waiting. So when you need help?" "Tonight and tomorrow." "Oh yeah, you think so?" "Yeah, because everything is packed up, so we will move the boxes tonight, and the furniture we will move tomorrow night." "Keisha, what you thinking about? You keep saying 'night.'" "Yes, Tony, we are moving at night. It's better, and plus, people don't be in your business."

"Okay, Ms. Keisha, so what time tonight?" "About seven to eight my friend will be there. Imma send the address to your phone." "Cool. I'll be there," Tony says. "Thanks, Tony, I deeply appreciate you," Keisha responds. Hanging up the phone, Keisha thanks God. Man, you are good and most faithful. As she walks into the hotel room, she says, "Ma, we have the help. All we need to do is go to the house and clean it before they come with our stuff." "Good, Kei, but before we leave, I have something to tell you." "What is it that you have to say, Ma?" "Your uncle passed away this morning." "What! Who, Uncle Jim?" Keisha asked, walking back and forth. "He died last night," Sheeba responds. "Oh, for real, and what happened to him?" "Well, the police said there was a robbery, and well, he was—" Sheeba begins to cry. "He was beaten." Keisha remains strong for Josh. "Ma, come on now, pull yourself together." "I'm trying to. Keisha, your uncle raised you. He was your father's best man. Listen, we come from far, that's all, he never left y'all out, never." "All right, Ma, do you think it has anything to do with Ang and them?" "Keisha, to be totally honest with you, I don't know. They are all in it together." "Damn, Ma, do you understand how serious this is? Who told you, Ma?" "Your Aunt Mya called me and gave me the news." "Damn, Ma, how is she doing? Uncle Jim was not in it like he used to be." "I know, Keisha, I know. But you know, I still can't come to grips with this shit. Keisha, I'm torn right now." "So, Ma, what, you think you need a break?" Keisha asks. "No, we need to get moving." "What did Kevin say? 'Cause I know you called him." "Kevin said everything is good over on his part." "What about Ang, Ma?" "Everybody is good. The newest problem is Uncle Jim." "Oh yeah, the newest problem is Uncle Jim, huh? Did you forget they have been watching our house?" "No, Keisha. No, Kevin said they will be getting to the bottom of it all. They will do what it takes to find out." "Ma, we will need to move out of state with this entire situation. I don't feel safe, Ma." "Yeah, Keisha, we're already moving far. What else do you want us to do?" Sheeba asks in tears. "Yeah, Ma, you're right. I'm thinking a lot right now, 'cause my car needs to be changed. You know, we could do that now; we could exchange it." "Keisha, what about the house?" "We could call a cleaning company to clean it. I have their number; all we need to do is set up an appointment." "Keisha, you always figure out how to take your mind off things." Keisha smiles. "Ma, it's not about keeping your mind off things; it's about what needs to be done. Plus, I need to get Josh into a new school. Who's to tell? They may follow him to school or have done so. Who knows?" "Keisha, you make sense. We need to tell Josh the truth, enough for him to understand we must move because of this and everything has to change." "Yeah, that's what I did not want to discuss, because I knew somehow he would be hurt." "He could invite his friends to the party, but after that he has to understand that he will not see them again." "Ma, it's not that serious. He could take their numbers, and they could do playdates. Look how big that house is; it's gigantic. To me, it's a lot bigger than our house." "You know, Keisha, you're right. We will do what we need to do. This whole Jim thing is getting to me I don't even know what I'm saying." "Come on, let's go, Josh. Let's go; we are going to get a new vehicle." "Great, Aunt Keisha, I'm excited for you," Josh says in a high-pitched voice. The three drive to the dealer. "Good morning," a tall gentleman greets them. "Hello, I'm interested in financing a vehicle." "Oh really, what vehicle do you have in mind?" the gentlemen asks. "Maybe an SUV. I was thinking a Dodge Durango, if possible." "Okay, we will have you fill out this form." "All right." Keisha sits and begins to fill out the form. "Wow, this is great, Aunt Keisha, you're gonna get a truck!" Josh exclaims. "Yeah, we will if I'm approved first. Excuse me, sir, here is my application," Keisha calls the man over to her. "Thanks, give me twenty minutes, and we will know if you're approved for a vehicle, much less your SUV." Keisha looked the man up and down. "Ma, does it seem like the man has an attitude, or is it just me?" "No, I think he has an attitude. Do you want to continue with him?" "I don't know. Let me see how he behaves further on. You know, I could call the cleaning company while we're waiting." Keisha gets on the phone. "Grandma, was Uncle Jim your brother?" "He was your grandpa's brother," Sheeba answers Josh. "Oh, well, does Grandpa know his brother died?" "No, not yet. He usually calls later in the day." "So are you going to tell him?" "Umm, I guess so. Really, I don't want to. Your Grandpa is locked up, and he will be there for a while. Telling him his brother passed will break his heart, but, Josh, I have to." "Grandma?" Josh says. "Yes, Josh, yes?" Sheeba answers. "Do you think my mom is coming home for my birthday?" "Huh, well, baby, there's a lot going on right now, so I'm unsure. You know, Josh, I could tell you that she will try her absolute best to help you. I mean to see you." "Is she in jail or something? Because this is the longest my mother has stayed away from me." "Yeah, Josh, I know if I could tell you something different, I would. Oh, the guy is coming back. Tell your Aunt Keisha to come back." Josh runs to Keisha. "Aunt Keisha, the man is back." "Oh, great! Now we can find out if we are approved." Keisha walks over to the guy. "Ms. Keisha Mayer, you have been approved." "Yes, yes, yes!" Keisha hugs her mother and nephew. Josh begins to dance. "You're excited, young boy," the gentleman says. "My interest is in the Dodge Durango. Do you have a silver or burgundy color?" "Yeah, we have silver, black, and merlot." "Oh, really? Get silver, Kei. Silver is easy to maintain," Sheeba advises her. "Well, I could get silver. That seems more reasonable to me." "All right, I will get the Durango pulled to the front. In the meantime please fill out the paperwork. On the paper you have your monthly payment, and today you need to put down five hundred dollars." "Okay, here is the money." Keisha hands the gentleman an envelope. "Please make sure you put your signature on each form. We went over the agreement, your monthly payment, and the warranty, and here is the packet informing you of the details about your Durango." "Well thank you. I will make sure to look over and fill out each form." The guy walks away. "All right, now I got my new whip pressed, we will prepare for our new place." Keisha smiles as she signs each form. The gentleman walks back to Keisha. "Ms. Mayer, are you ready to see your new Dodge?" "Yes, I am, but before we go further, I would like to test-drive it," Keisha expresses. They walk to the front of the building. "Oh, here are the keys to my vehicle." Keisha and the sell man exchange keys. "I will be right back," Keisha assures the man. She turns on the ignition and begins driving around the block. When arriving back to the dealership Keisha thanks the man. "Thank you for taking the tags off. Give me five minutes," she says to the man. Keisha begins taking her things out of her old car and placing them in the new SUV. "Come on, Josh, get in. Thanks, sir, have a wonderful day." Keisha gets in the Durango. "Next move, Ma, we are headed to the new house." Keisha feels relieved as she drives off. The people helping them move should be getting to the house in the next hour and a half. The whole vehicle process took about two hours, which seems like a lot of time. "Well, Kei, our day has been spent well." "Did you check on Kevin, Ma?" Keisha asks. "No, he will call." "Did you tell him we were moving?" "Yeah, he said to not sell the house yet. Wait a little and they will tell us when to sell." "Oh, interesting, they don't need the money, Ma." "Keisha, they have a point. Just follow their lead, okay?" "All right, Ma, whatever. So, with that being said, we should keep the furniture in there and get all new stuff." "You know what, Keisha, do what you want, 'cause none of this shit make sense anyway." They arrived at the new house after Keisha stopped and bought a futon for them to sit on. The furniture warehouse made same-day delivery to help Keisha out. The only things available were their futons, so Keisha brought two. "Well, we won't have our living room and dining room set until two weeks from now," Keisha says calmly. "We will sleep on the futons until we get our beds." "Aunt Keisha, we have a nice home. That's what matters

to me," Josh says. Keisha's phone rings. "Hello, yes, this is her...
Oh, okay, I will open the door." The people from the cleaning
company came in. "Hello, good afternoon. Thank you for coming. Ma, sit down. We have to relax, because when the things get
here, we will have to take time and unpack." "Keisha, you should
have them clean the other house as well." "Ma, you're right, that
is a good idea," Keisha says, smiling. Sheeba's phone rings. "Oh,
man, this is your dad." Sheeba answers the phone. She pauses
for a minute. "Hello, what's up, Jerome? I don't know how to say
this, but hey, Jim was beaten to death. He is gone, he is gone."
Sheeba begins to cry. "Yeah, he died last night. They say it's robbery...We will find out. Did you talk to Ang?...Oh, you did. What
she say?...Man, out here a lot been taking place...Yeah, I'm glad
your time is decreasing, because you need to talk some sense
into your kids. People out here dying. Honey, I know the shit
ain't changed...What, you trying to lose your kids?...No, I need
you to understand. You not making any sense on these calls,
Jerome, what will that do? Anyway, you don't have long. Keisha,
come talk to your dad." Sheeba hands her the phone. "Hey,
Dad...Not so good. We had to move, Uncle Jim died, people
been following me...Yes, Dad, they're after Ang, yeah, we had to
move...Yeah, you taught me that, Dad, I got it with me at all
times...Yes, Dad, but I'll only use it if I have to, like life and
death situations...Yes, Dad, yes, I know...Yes, I love you, too, and
I'll make sure, Dad...I know, make sure...Love you too." Keisha
hangs up the phone. "Ma, I love my dad, but he is crazy." She
laughs. "He said, 'Remember what I taught you.' He advises me
to visit the range. My dad is crazy. But hey, I gotta protect my
own, you know." "Yeah, we have to do what we have to do, Kei,
it's survival. This stuff is crazy. Well, we are doing the safe way,
which to me is better anyway." Josh walks around, exploring the
house. "The people are done with the house, Aunt Keisha." "Oh,
yes, ma'am, here is your pay. I will be calling you all again; I have
another place that needs cleaning." Keisha walks them to the

door. "Thank you again. You all did a great job. At least I know that already." She sits down on the futon. Yes, I will relax before Jas comes. Keisha falls asleep on the futon.

CHAPTER 7

THE MOVE

"Keisha! Keisha!" Sheeba calls as Keisha tosses and turns on the futon. "Yes," she answers softly. "Wake up; Jasmine and Tony are on their way." "Wait, hold up, what?" Keisha jumps up. "Yeah, get up. We have to keep moving. I'm sure you got enough rest," Sheeba responds. "Damn, I must've been asleep awhile." "Yeah, Kei, you have been sleeping. Josh and me went to the park; we walked the neighborhood. We even gone to the store, girl, while you slept." "Man, I can't believe it! I was supposed to take a quick nap. Did they say how far they were?" "No, but they are on their way," Sheeba says. "All we can do is wait. Stacy said tomorrow she will be coming by." "For real, Ma?" "Yeah, she wants to help unpack. Plus, Josh can play with Ryan." "Yeah, you're right. There's a list of things to do, Ma. Did you call the cable company?" "Yeah, I did that when we were approved." "Oh, so they should be coming soon." "Keisha, I told you Monday, and you said we could use our phones and tablet till then, remember?" "Oh yeah, that's right. You see, Ma, I'm just trying to keep it together." "Kei, that is you. I know when too much is on your head. We will soon be finished with all of this, you know. When we're finished, Kei, we can celebrate, and you can relax." "Yeah, I guess, because having a break really matters, especially when your body feels overworked." Someone knocks at the door, and Keisha walks over to open it. "Oh hey, what's up?" she says. "Hi, pretty face, looking at you lightens up my day." "Oh yeah, and I guess that is how you're trying to make my day, huh." He laughs. "You know what's up, Keisha. I'm still waiting on my date." "Tony, you can put all the boxes that say 'living room' and 'kitchen' right over there. The boxes that say 'bedroom,' just put them upstairs," Keisha says in the sweetest voice. "Thank you, Tony, I'm really grateful." "No biggy, beautiful." Keisha smiles at Tony's response. "Girl, when I say these men can work and they move fast, Keisha, you know," Jasmine says, walking into the house. "Oh, mi love this." "Yeah, you like it?" "Keisha, it nice for real, me nah lie," Jasmine compliments. "Anyway, how you look so sleepy? You mussi just wake." (You just woke up) "Yeah, Jas, I just woke up, and I'm still sleepy, but yeah, things have to be done," Keisha responds. "Well, you know how that goes. Did you hear about Carl?" Jas asks. "No, girl, I have not spoke to anyone. From packing to these men watching the house and trying to get shit together, time to talk doesn't exist." "Well, Carl got locked up, and di people, dem is saying his sister snitched. Anymore, me ah tell yuh, people can't be trusted," Jas expresses. "Dang, and I was going to ask Carl to help me with some things around the house." "Girl, that can't happen now. No more discounts; you just have to spend your money. You was going to put some security cameras in here?" Jas asks. "Yes, because people can't be trusted," Keisha responds. "Anyway, come give me a hug. I missed you." Keisha hugs Jasmine. "Stacy and Tasha said they coming to help you set up. I was thinking we should do a woman's sleepover or weekend party so we are able to set up and be done with your house, you know," Jasmine suggests. "Jasmine, I have to tell you, you're extremely smart. That's a good idea. I have no furniture yet, but we could dress the walls, put the clothes up, and you know, do things around the furniture." "Yes, girl, all you have to do is get some beds, and we just camp out, you know?" Keisha smiles. "That's why you're my best friend: you always have good things to say and great ideas." "We do it for each other. I love you," Jasmine says, giving Keisha another hug. "You know, when all this is over, we have to go out. We could even go to New York and party if you don't feel safe over here." "You know, I'll take you up on that offer." "Excuse me, ladies, we are basically finished, so I guess I'll see you tomorrow again." "Yeah, but tomorrow we are just moving the bedroom sets. Everything else will stay." "Oh, that sounds quick. I'll get another truck so it's one trip," Tony suggests. "That's nice. How much does it cost?" Keisha asks. "Oh, sweetheart, you don't have to pay me; I'm here to help." "Tony, I don't want this to be your problem," Keisha responds. "Naw, it's not, Keisha. Trust me, that is the least I could do," Tony replies. Keisha rolls her eyes. "You're good to me, Tony. I ain't asked you for help, and you still insist on helping me." Jasmine adds, "Yuh nuh, see, when man want yuh, make him spend money." "Jas, yuh love talk," Tony responds. "Wait, Tony, you Jamaican?" Keisha asks. "No, well, somewhat?" "What is 'somewhat'?" Keisha asks. "The story is long. Let me make it short: my mother is American, and my father is Jamaican." "Oh, so you can speak Patwa." "Yeah, because I grew up with my father's mother. My grandmother raised me, and she is totally Jamaican." "Oh, interesting," Keisha says with a bright smile. "Yeah, that's it, you know," Tony says as he slowly walks away. "Tony, thank you." Keisha walks him to the door. "I'll see you tomorrow." She gives him a hug. "Thanks, everyone. Tomorrow we will have your funds," Keisha assures the three guys. She shuts the door. "Jasmine, you staying?" "Girl, yes, we could drink, and I got some food here. You're good; we could talk and things like that." "Jasmine, you're a great friend, I'm telling you." Jasmine pours the drinks. "Mama Sheeba, you want some Hennessy?" Jasmine asks. "You already know the answer to that, my love," Sheeba responds. The girls sit in the kitchen discussing hard times, having to move, her uncle dying, and her sister not coming around. "Hold on, let me give Mama the drink." Jasmine walks to the back room and gives Sheeba the drink. "Yes, my girl talk the things them now," Jasmine says. (Tell me everything) "Keisha, you don't have to worry about nothing, because one, you're strong, and two, you're always going to make sure people are fine. Once you take care of yourself and your family, sincerely, you will be fine. There is no need to stress about anything. You know, you need a man." "Jasmine, a man is not on my mind right now." "Oh, for real? Well, when you feel the need, you need to get one to keep you stress free." "Jasmine, men bring stress, not help stress." They both laugh. "Girl, you're independent, hardworking, and don't ask no one for things, so men can't bring stress to you. If anything, you bring stress to them." "Girl, shut up," Keisha responds, laughing. "That's one thing you'll make me do: laugh, Jasmine. You know, for sure we have to party after this, you know?" The women go to sleep after their long talk about life. Of course, Keisha first made sure Josh was all right. The day was exhausting for Josh, so he went to bed right away. The following morning, Keisha wakes up and goes to the grocery store. She packs her house with food, preparing for her girlfriends to come over. Sheeba cleans out the fridge, and Jasmine began helping Josh set up his room, putting the clothes away. "Aunt Jasmine, have you spoke to my mother?" Josh asks. "No, why?" "I miss her. She has not called or anything, and these guys are looking for Uncle Kevin. Did you know Uncle Kevin is my mom's favorite brother?" "What? Who told you that, Josh?" "She always says that she always calls Kevin 'the leading king.'" Josh laughs. "Well, with all that being said, he must be her favorite for real." "My birthday is coming up," Josh says. "Yes, we are going to have a bomb party for you, and you know your mother never misses your parties or birthday. She will come through. But sometimes people are busy, Josh." "Too busy for me? That is okay, I guess," Josh replies. "Look at that, Josh, your room is done. Now when your bedroom set comes, we will put your games up on your shelf, you know." "Yes, Aunt Jasmine." "Let us go check on your grandma. Seems like she is cooking. Mama Sheeba!" Jasmine calls out. "Yeah?" "Oh, you're up here. Wow, your room is big." "You think so?" Sheeba says. "Of course, look at it: you have to step up in your room. It almost looks like two levels. Oh, your walk-in closet is great." "Yeah, it's nice up here," Sheeba responds. "Well, we're up here to help you put away your clothes and stuff." "Oh, thanks, because all that packing at the house got me tired." "I know, so how you like your clothes?" "Jasmine, it don't matter. Just put all my pants and skirts on one side and all my dresses and tops on the other side." "That's different. I usually put my clothes in order by color." "Yeah, the color stuff is a bit much. I like to get to my pants, so I'm not going to put things all together; I like to separate them." "Oh, that's still good. You have some sort of order." Jasmine smiles. "When the girls come, the house will be organized and neat in no time. Keisha must be the one cooking, huh." "Yeah, she is making breakfast. Josh, take this box and put it by the bathroom. Put all the soap on the bottom shelf in the closet. I will put the bathroom rugs and curtains up myself." "All right, Grandma." Josh begin unpacking the soaps and lotions on the bottom shelf. "Grandma, you have a lot of soaps. They can't fit on one shelf." "Yes, I know, Josh. don't put the lotion on the shelf. When my furniture comes, I will put my lotion on the dresser. You already know how I set my things up, Josh. We will start with what we need to, and everything will go right into place." "That's good," Jasmine responds. "Josh's room is all unpacked; he just needs his room set for it to be complete." "Jasmine, baby, thank you," Sheeba says with joy in her voice. "You see, the more, the merrier." "Yes, because when there's a team, things get done much quicker. We've known each other a long time in order to help each other out. Keisha's been my friend since school days." "Yes, so you know what she's like." "The truth is Keisha and I like some of the same things; we should have been sisters." Jasmine laughs. "Well, my work here is done," she says, walking out of the room. "Thanks, Jas, I appreciate you," Sheeba replies. "I'm going to finish up my room." "All right," Jasmine says while walking down the steps. "Keisha, baby, upstairs is almost done, unless you're going to decorate the hallway." "Yeah, but that's simple. It's the same things. Stacy can help with that, girl, relax; you helped Josh and Ma." "You know, they both got mad clothes." "Yo, Jas, you think we could go to the gun range?" "Hell yeah, that's all the way me. You better not tell Stacy; she going to be against it." "Please she could keep the boys and we could go. My dad said I need to sharpen up. I know what that means." Jas laughs. "Yeah, you know, Jerome is a madhead already, you done know (You already know). I mean, with these guys following people, I have to stay strapped, 'cause it won't be me. Keisha, you stay far from the fuckery. So to protect you, as I said, ain't bad. I got you; you know I do. This food is good." The doorbell rings. "Stacy, baby, what's up?" Jas says with the biggest smile on her face. "Hey, J, what's up?" Stacy kisses her on the forehead. "Tasha, look at you, girl. You look good, so good." "Jasmine, stop nuh, man," Tasha responds. "You know when you show up, thing's ah guh nice," Jasmine compliments Tasha. "Yeah, that's what you always say." The ladies go upstairs to say hi to Sheeba. "Hey, girls, what's going on?" she says. "Tasha, it's been a while." "Yes, I know it's been a while." "You make me laugh, because you know, and still it's a while. How is your mother doing? You know your Uncle Jim passed away?" "Yes, I know. It's all so sudden; I can't even bother to get into that. Jeff know and Jim know them supposed to link up. The shit ain't going down like that somebody haffi dead (Someone has to die). Aunt Sheeba, make we talk (Let's talk) 'bout getting this house together," Tasha says to her aunt. Tasha and Keisha are cousins because of her Father Jerome. "You're right, because I can't stop thinking about it.

Truly, it's been on my mind like crazy." "Aunt Sheeba, nuh worry 'bout that. The ah guh take care of it." Tasha hugs Sheeba as tears fall from both of their eyes. "Let us focus on getting this house together." Josh walks in the room. "Grandma, here is your breakfast." He hands her the plate. "Thank you, baby. Hi, Ryan, come give grandma a kiss." Ryan runs over and gives her a kiss. "Nice to see you again. I missed you, baby. You should have some fun. Josh is getting his stuff today, and we will fix up his room," Sheeba expresses. "Anyhow, Mama, we're going down now to figure out what Keisha want us to do," Jasmine says. Jasmine, Keisha's best friend from middle school, is also Jamaican. "Hey, Keisha, what's next?" the ladies ask. "Are y'all hungry?" "Yeah." "Well here is your food. I made some coffee and put a shot of Henny in it. Enjoy." "Damn, you starting early," says Tasha. "Easy does it, cuz, easy does it," Keisha responds. The ladies laugh, talk, and eat. After breakfast they begin to unpack. Stacy is in charge of putting up the décor on the walls. Tasha, Keisha, and Jasmine fix up the basement, putting one futon downstairs. "Keisha, your room is going to be in the basement?" Stacy ask. "Yes, girl, it's like having my own apartment, and you see how big the room is down there." "Yes, I see it's nice, man, nice. Mi love this house, yah," Tasha compliments. "You know, what if you ever have someone come over? Josh wouldn't know, because you have so many entrances, like two on the side and down here," Jasmine adds. "Yes, that's why I took the basement." "Oh, and you have another room down here." "Yeah, I know, girl, this house is nice. I love it." "Well, this calls for a celebration." "Listen, Jasmine said it first." Keisha laughs. "After Josh's party, we could party," Tasha adds. "Yeah, but I want to see how this warring shit goes." "Keisha, Justin, dem have it. They know what's going on, and they are handling it," Tasha responds. The ladies put things up, and after they finished, they cleaned up the boxes and put them by the side of the house. "Keisha, it's time to rest," Stacy says with a smile. "Yeah, girl, we put in a lot of work," Tasha comments. "What time is it, anyway?" Keisha asks. "It's about four," Jasmine answers. "We have time before Tony and the men arrive," Keisha notes. "Hey y'all, wanna go for a ride?" "Hell yeah, why not." "All right, let's shower and get ready." "There's three full bathrooms in here; we all could shower and get ready at the same time," Jasmine adds. "Girl, I feel so indefatigable." "Keisha, how could you feel tireless and you been overworked?" "Not really, because you ladies came through and made it better for us." Keisha smiles. The women all take a shower, get dressed, and head out. "Ma, we are leaving. Do you want anything from the store?" "No, I think it is all covered. Are you going to be long?" Sheeba asks. "No, maybe two hours at the most," Keisha responds. "All right, then we are good," Sheeba reassures her. The women walk out of the house. Keisha presses her unlock button on her key. "Wait one minute. Who has that Durango?" Jasmine asks. Keisha smiles, looking back at her. "Get in, ladies." "Man, this truck drives nice, though," Tasha compliments. "I wish you didn't have to give it back." "Give what back?" Jasmine replies. "It looks like sah a new truck she has." "We don't know that; she still did not answer we." "Yeah, you're right about that. Keisha, is this your Durango?" Jasmine asks with sass. "Yeah, it is. I had to change it up on them. If these niggas watchin' me, I need to be anonymous on their asses, and that's the real deal." "Oh, me see now. Smart, boo, I'm not tellin' no lie, I rate you," Jasmine compliments. "Where are you going?" "I want to see if they're watchin' the house still." "Why, Kei? Why would you do that?" Stacy asks, concerned. "Stacy, we have to know, because I don't want them following the guys to the new house." Tasha laughs. "So yesterday did you do the same thing?" "No, I told Jasmine what the vehicle looks like." "So why can't you do that again today?" "Huh, I am unsure; guess I just want to see for myself. After that, we will go to the rug store so I can get a couple of area rugs for the living and dining rooms. What do you think about the dining area?"

"Yeah, you could fix it up nice, because it is not like y'all going to eat in there. Knowing y'all, most likely you are going to eat in the kitchen," Jasmine responds. "Okay, then I will get three rugs instead so I can pretty up the dining room too," Keisha agrees. "What is the set color for the house?" Stacy asks. "You know the walls are gray on the main floor, so I'm thinking burgundy and maybe an ivory dining room set." "Keisha, you always get burgundy." "Well I ain't Keisha if that color is not somewhere around." They all laugh. "You right for sure. Things seem so odd, but you know we will push through this; we always do." "Keisha, it's like you run a joke, and then your mind goes right back on the problem." "Tasha, do you know how it feels to be having to go through so much?" Keisha asks. Tears fall from her eyes. "Man, I only know the half. We don't get in them problems here. Uncle Jim ah the biggest problem right now." "Yo, Tasha, Ang is the middle of the problem, and that answers it all. She is my sister, and she is moving really reckless. The thing about it is I gotta keep all the bullshit together, as they claim to say they are keeping the problem intact," Keisha expresses. "Welp, we here," Jasmine announces. "You see any gray van?" "No, but when we passed three houses down, I seen one." "Oh, you think it's them?" Stacy asks to frighten everyone. "How could I know?" Keisha responds. "How 'bout we drive back around, park, and walk past as if we are strolling the neighborhood. We could walk down to kind of look in the vehicle to see if people are in the van." "Oh yes, and get a better look. You know we hot ladies already; if it's men, them ah guh try look we," Jasmine suggests. "Tasha and Jasmine go, because they will not know y'all. Stacy is a liability 'cause she's Kevin's girl." "Well all right, then meet us on the next block." The ladies jump out of the SUV. "Okay, let's go." Keisha drives off, turning the corner quickly. "Keisha, this is not a good idea." "What you mean, Stacy? Jasmine and Tasha will play their cards right. If anything, we could even get a good description and nail these fuckers." "You know, you're right. Let me clam down." Keisha parks the truck. "Something said ride past the house. The way them niggas approached me in the restaurant prior to all this crazy shit, I swear they was out to kill me. Look, we have to; I mean have to beat them at their own game. Stacy, I want to go back to having a peaceful life."

CHAPTER 8

TO SETTLE

The ladies come back to the truck. "Hey, open up." Jasmine bangs on the door. "Hurry up, drive!" Tasha shouts. "Why y'all so extra?" "Girl, I got their number and am supposed to tell you one of them niggas is friends with Kevin's people." "Hold on, what people of Kevin?" Stacy asks. "That dude he always used to chill with all the time, Stacy. I just can't member his name, but he used to stay with him. He was light-skinned with cornrows. Stacy, they don't be with each other again like that; that dude been missing in action for a while. You know who I'm talking about. I just can't remember his name." "Did he recognize you?" "I don't know, plus I had a hat." "So did y'all talk much?" Keisha asks. "Not much but I have his number," Tasha responds. "Damn, so what we going to do?" Stacy says. "Look, easy, we could stray them away from watching the house. We could call them and have them meet us some place." "Sounds like a good plan." "Y'all need to be safe. What if they spot you, Tasha?" "Please, we just meeting up. I ain't getting out of the vehicle." "Man, that's risky as shit, but the move needs to happen, and these niggas don't need to know where I live now." "We got you, sis, don't fret. It's a good thing you felt that shit; could you imagine they see you moving shit out of the house?" "Yeah, I'm glad I stopped by. Well, now I know we will have a clear move." "Yeah, call Tony and see if he can get all your furniture except the living room set. Oh yes, and the dining room set as well. Have Stacy wear a hat and go in just in case." "Everything ain't clear yet until we move the things out, and you know that ain't nobody following us." "You're right." Keisha drives back home. "We could get the rugs tomorrow; I'm nervous now." "Kei, stop that. We got you. I told them to meet us up by the mall, which is a good distance from where you're staying at." "Okay, call me on the way back." "We will." The two ladies leave and go their separate ways. Tony and the guys pick up the furniture from the old house. Everything goes as planned. Keisha is able to get her things out of the house and the ladies are fine. Saturday goes well; she pays the movers and sits with the ladies, discussing the experience with the men. "Tell me what went down when y'all met up with them." "Oh, we went to the park, walked around talking and shit," Tasha explains. "So what was that guy with them?" Stacy asks. "Who, Paul, the guy I said was always with Kevin?" "Yeah, him, was he with them?" "Naw, they dropped him off." "That name, Paul, sounds so familiar," Stacy adds, trying to remember. "Well, that's a plus he was not there with them. Okay, so tell me what happened," Keisha insists. "Nothing, really. He asked basic questions, such as where I am from. I told him Florida." The ladies laugh as Tasha continues to spell out the information. "He said he wants to get to know me or whatever." "So what, are you going to continue talking to him?" Keisha asks. "Yeah, most likely, but he will never know the real me. I will give him the butter me." "What is the butter you?" "Girl, anything that sweet him. I have my plans. I asked him if he was from where I met him at," Tasha continues. "Oh, for real, what did he say?" Stacy asks. "He said he was waiting on a friend, but he is not from around that area. I played it well and was like, You know Jeff? He was like, No.

So, we continued talking. He was like, he was on a run for one of his friends. Girl, I'm going to move in closer to him, you know. So I can find out everything." "Well, did he ask you if you're from that area?" "I told him my cousin lives on the next block, and we were just walking." "Damn, Tasha, you are super smart, girl. You are playing the game right." "Well, we're getting to the bottom of this crap. Seriously, they killed my Uncle Jim. That ain't sitting right with me, so I'm doing my part." "We don't know if they killed Uncle Jim as yet." "Well, they are following you; something ain't right. He did say Paul got some things to take care. So I don't know what that means, but I know we shall find out." "Jasmine, what about the nigga you were talking to?" "Keisha, mi nah lie, ah real dog shit that." Keisha laughs as Jasmine continues to describe that man's character. "His idiotic ass try to fuck. I was like, nigga, I know you from nowhere. He is talking shit, like man, ease my day, ease it for me. Honestly, I feel like if he were in his own car, he would have tried something. But, Kei, he knows how that would of end up. Girl I had to run him outta my car. He was acting bad." The ladies continue to laugh. "So one has somewhat of sense and the other one don't have none." The ladies laugh at Keisha's comment. "So on the other hand, Tony has been completely helpful. He set up the bedroom furniture in everyone's rooms. He asked his nephew and cousin for assistance. I felt extremely grateful and excited. I owe him a date; he did not take pay from me. I paid his cousin and nephew, though. He would not take money from me at all." "So you owe him a date, huh? That is a whole other story," Jasmine responds. "I'm trying to go to a trove store," Keisha comments. "Girl, you always want to go to the store that has the most valuable things. You love the finer things in life, right?" "Yes, I do, because things like that last a lot longer. Don't act surprised. Also, it is like having treasure in your home," Keisha explains. The ladies end their day by celebrating and enjoying their time spent together. The next day they go out and buy area rugs for the house. Keisha also purchases her dining room set. "Thank God I have you girls, because to be truthful, it would have taken a lot longer to set up our new home." After shopping the ladies go back to Keisha's house. They dance, talk, eat good food, and drink nice liquor. Night comes down, and it is now time for the girls to end their friends' weekend. "Kei, girl, I'm telling you, this weekend was a joy. Even though we worked a bit, I still had fun," Jasmine compliments. "Yeah, I would have to agree with Jas," Stacy and Tasha comment. The ladies leave, and Keisha immediately begins getting ready for the week. Her phone rings. "Hey, Stacy, what happened; did you forget something?" "No, I wanted to tell you I will be coming back on Thursday to help you out around the house." Keisha feels grateful. "Thanks, I appreciate you. This whole time I did not have to go through much, because you all were there to help me out all the way through. We are set. It's just time for the party on Saturday. I am excited. Oh yes, don't forget to bring your jersey. I'm going to remind the other ladies as well." Keisha hangs up the phone.

CHAPTER 9
GETTING TO KNOW YOU

The first workweek in the new house feels great. Every morning Keisha wakes up one hour early, making sure she gets Josh to school on time. Her days are a bit longer, because now she is in charge of picking Josh up from his friend's house. Everything seems to be going well. Thursday morning Josh asks Keisha to call his mother. "Josh, we will have to call her when you get home from school." Keisha pulls into the school driveway. "Josh, baby, have a good day. I love you." Keisha blows him a kiss. Josh looks at her, smiling. He walks to the school building. "Damn, Ang is sending the funds but still not calling. I don't even know how to reach her." She begins crying, thinking about all the changes that have taken place in their life. She picks up the phone and calls her brother Kevin. "Hey, Kevin, could you let me know about what's taking place with Ang?" "Keisha, Ang is good." "All right, then she got to know Josh's birthday is coming up." "Yeah, we got that on lock, Kei; all you gotta do is take care of Josh, Kei!" Kevin yells into the phone. "All right, Kevin, whatever, since being concerned about my sister is a damn crime." Keisha hangs up the phone. I don't even know where to start. This shit is crazy. When Keisha gets to work, she begins looking up information on the guys that Tasha told her about. She has the license plate number and one of the guys' name. Tasha has been talking to the guy almost every day. All Keisha can think about is keeping her family safe. So much is going on: the guys are still watching the old house, Angie is still avoiding her family, and Josh is still yearning for his mother. Keisha feels overwhelmed all over again. The only thing going right is the party. The decorations, food, invites, and everything else are set for Saturday. Josh is about to have one of the best moments in his life. Keisha is sick of crying about the things that are out of place in her life. She remembers what Tony said about calling him if she needed to talk. She picks up the phone and calls him. "Hey, Tony," Keisha says when he answers. "Hey, what's up, Keisha? We spoke one time this week," Tony reminds her. "Yes, I know. What, you don't want to talk?" "Keisha, I would talk to you every day; you know that too." She smiles. "Yes, but now we need to talk because it's been days since we talked." "So that is how it will work nowadays." Keisha laughs. "Well honestly, I wanted you to stop by the house." "And you already know that is a yes." Keisha laughs again. "Okay, when you get off, stop by my house. We could talk and get to know each other." "I got you. So I'll hit you up, all right?" They hang up, and Keisha continues with her workday. While walking to her truck, she gets a phone call. "Hello," Keisha answers. "Yes, Ma?" "Before coming home stop by the store. We need to have enough food for Stacy and Ryan. Remember, they are coming today," Sheeba reminds Keisha. "All right, Ma, I will do that." "Oh, and the neighbor said someone has been snooping around the house, looking in the windows." "For real? I know that they were still watching the house, but what is the sense to look in the windows? These people are crazy. They need to hurry up and do something, seriously. Today has been crazy, Ma: Josh asking me to call Ang, Kevin's little outburst, and now this shit. It just seems so hectic right now, I

can't be bothered." "Don't stress, baby girl, that's the old house.
They can snoop around all they want. Things will get better
soon, trust that," Sheeba reassures her. Keisha goes to pick her
nephew up from his friend's house. After picking Josh up, she
heads to the grocery store to buy some food. "How was your day
in school, Josh?" "It was good. I told my friends we moved. Oh,
and all of my friends are coming to the party. I'm excited, Aunt
Keisha." "That's good, Josh, I'm happy too. Can't wait to see
your face on your party day." "Aunt Keisha, the school year just
started, and we moved far away. Will I change schools?" "I am
still thinking about that. What, you don't want to?" "No, Aunt
Keisha, I don't want to." "Okay, Josh, I hear you, but I can't
promise you that. Josh, you know once words like that come out
of my mouth it must be serious." Josh stays quiet as Keisha continues to talk about safety and love. When they arrive at their
new house, Keisha calls, "Yes, I'm home. Hey, Ma, thanks for all
that you do." "Keisha, keep it up, you hear?" Sheeba warns
Keisha about her sassy comment. "What are you doing with that,
Josh? Go in the house." Sheeba looks at Josh holding a box in
his hand. "Grandma, it is for my school project," Josh responds
as he enters the house. "Man, today was so fun, Grandma," he
expresses. "Can't wait until my party. It's about to be lit." Sheeba
smiles. "I cannot wait, either, Josh. You're going to be double
digits." Josh smiles and runs up the stairs to his room. "Ma, my
friend is stopping by. I'm going to get in the shower. If he comes
let him in," Keisha informs her mother. "Oh, okay." Sheeba
looks at Keisha with surprise on her face. Running down the
steps, Keisha sings, "You have just a rocket to da moon." She
sings the song so much, she decides to play it on her speaker.
Getting in the shower, she thanks God for everything he is doing
for her. "Only thing now is to settle in and trust you now, Lord,"
Keisha says aloud. She hears Stacy calling her name. "Kei! Kei!"
"Yes, I'm in the shower." "Oh, well, your phone is ringing, and
Tony is here." "What? Okay, tell him I'm getting ready," Keisha

says, shocked. She rushes to finish her shower. Oh, damn, this man moves fast, she thinks. Entering her room, Keisha quickly dries her body off. Shit, I ain't 'bout to dress up. It's not time for that yet. She throws on some sweatpants and a tight top. Looking in the mirror, she smiles and says, "Who am I fooling? I'm not trying to impress anyone." She laughs and puts on her lip gloss. "Oh, hell, I'll just put on some neutral eye shadow just to give my face a little glow." She slides her feet into her fluffy bedroom slippers. Walking up the steps, she says to herself, "Damn, I wonder if Tony is mad at me." "Good evening," Keisha says as she enters the living room. "Hey, sexy," Tony says. Keisha laughs. "Hey, what's up, Tony? Ma and Stacy, I'll be back. Come on, Tony, let's go," Keisha says, walking toward the front door. "All right, Ms. Sheeba, Stacy, you done know (you already know)," Tony says as he quickly walks behind Keisha. "So, where we going out, Keisha?" "Oh, we going to my truck. We could sit and talk, you know. All right, we could do that, it's whatever." The two walk to her truck. "Man, that's your truck? Keisha, you're sexy driving that, love." "Well thank you, and how many times you gonna call me sexy?" She smiles. "Damn, if I could tell you every day, I would," Tony replies. "Yeah, so what is sexy about me?" "Huh, what you mean, Keisha? Everything—your eyes, your body, your shape. You don't see you have a body on you." "Yes, I know all what you sayin'. I just want to hear it from you," Keisha replies. "Well there it goes. I said it. Oh, and your voice is like that, girl; you sexy, that's it." Keisha laughs. "So you got any kids?" "Yeah, I have a daughter. She is three." "Oh, just asking." Keisha gets quiet. "What's up, Keisha, what you be doing?" "Nothing. Working, trying to take care of my family. Every now and then, me and my girls been going out, you know." "Oh, well, we could do that too," Tony suggests. "Yes, I'm okay with going out with you, but there's a lot of things going on right now." "I feel like that's an excuse, because you moved, your house is set up, and the party is basically set. So what is one date? Girl, you be bullshittin' for real." "Naw, we are going to go out. Tony, if I was bullshittin', would I be talking to you now?" "Yeah, you might be bored." "No, not at all. Remember, Josh's party is Saturday. After that we could go out, you know." "All right, I'll keep you to your word." Keisha smiles. "If I'm worth it, then you will wait." Tony laughs. "I see what you hittin' me with, girl. Tell me this: do you want to get to know me?" "If I didn't, would I keep telling you that we would go out on a date?" "People say anything these days." "Yes, Tony, but I'm not. Why would I do that and show you my house? Please, and I even invited you to Josh's party." "All right, fine, no pressure. When a man sees something they really want, they go after, you know." "Yeah, sounds good. We could still talk though." "Oh, so you're saying we could talk every day now." He smiles, looking Keisha in the eyes. "Yes, I mean, if it's something you look forward to," Keisha says. "Come here." She smiles. "I am already here." "Could I give you a kiss?" "Huh." Keisha pauses. He kisses her. She does not pull back; she kisses him back. "Woah, damn," Keisha says after kissing him. "You know how to kiss." He laughs. "And your lips are sexy and soft. Damn, girl, I cannot get you off my head, and it coming like mi make it worse now." (It's worst now) Keisha laughs. "Tony, I ain't asked you to kiss me; you took that kiss." "Keisha, you have to be my girl." "Tony, slow down, because we need to get to know each other before saying we gonna be together." "All right, so what now?" "I will call you, and the phone works both ways—we could call each other," Keisha says proudly. "Fine, that's not a problem. I was waiting for you to give me permission, that's all, baby girl. Okay, so let me walk you to your door." "Sure, let us go," Keisha says, getting out of the truck. She closes her door as Tony closes his. She presses the alarm on her key and walks with Tony to her house. "Keisha, I'm not gonna lie I'm attracted to you. Every time you're around, I just feel really hot. You know, you're well worth the wait." "You know what, Imma give you another kiss for that." She kisses him.

"Thanks for walking me to the door. Call me when you get home." "Okay, I will do that," Tony responds. Keisha walks in the house. "Stacy, what's up?" "Nothing, just relaxing. I made sure the boys took a shower. When is your living room set coming?" "The people said two weeks, so I am guessing sometime next week." "Yeah, that is good. You know, I haven't seen Kevin in like two weeks. Kei, he has never waited this long to come by." "Stacy, the good thing about this is the fact the people have yet to follow you home. That's the good thing about it, you know." "Boy, I tell you, I miss him, because we always used to be together before this shit started." "Girl, do you remember who the Paul guy is now?" "Yeah, I do, when I come to think of it. Well, Paul is the one who created all this drama. Seriously, Keisha." Stacy pauses and begins staring at the wall. "Stacy, hello, you just blanked out for a minute." "You know, it's not necessarily blanking out; it's...well, Paul used to be close to Kevin. The crazy thing about it is I still talk to his girlfriend." "Hold the fuck up. What?" Keisha asks aggressively. "Does she ask you questions about things?" "No, not really, but I'm unsure as to what she may do now." "Girl, don't cut her off, but play smooth. Talk to her still, but don't let her know nothing. The thing is you tell her stuff, you know how that goes. If you pull away, they will know you caught on to them." "Keisha, think about it. Kevin knows Paul's shady; that is why he ain't around no more, right?" "Yes, but still, think about it. Say they know that Kevin don't disclose with you. Listen, these people know how secretive our family is." "Yeah, that is right, he probably told his girl, you know." "Another thing is it may all be a plot. Until all this shit is over with, we could play the game they play, you know." "Keisha, I am glad y'all found out who is behind all this. Man, this is so confusing. Paul don't even seem to be grimy and now look at this crap. Alisha been talking to me normal, even setting up playdates." "Stacy, do not be alarmed; that's the way the game goes. Growing up I saw my dad, uncles, and even siblings fight so many people.

You see, that thing called money is well needed and can cause enemies, can cause greed—all types of greed, all types of shit. Girl, anyone could switch what they do. Stacy, it's cold, so being in a relationship with Kevin could have lots of love, but never get the game twisted. Girl, you will see people come and go. Don't get close to them; get close to your man with hopes it don't change him." Keisha rubs Stacy's back. "Dry your tears, baby, you just need to take care of you and yours, all right?" Keisha continues to support Stacy in her emotional state. The phone rings. "Oh, it's Kevin. See, look at that!" Keisha answers the phone. "Hey, what's up, bro?...Oh, you called to apologize for your nasty ass attitude. Well, I already forgive you, memba; you're fully me." Keisha laughs. "Anyway, what you doing now?... Oh, Stacy is with me. She's gonna be with me until the shit calms down; she don't wanna be alone...No problem, we good. That's what family does...Hold on, yeah, love you too." Keisha hands Stacy the phone. She sits on her futon thinking about what Tony said to her in the truck. I don't know, honestly; I feel I should give him a chance, but you know, it is going to be after he shows me what he is all about, Keisha considers in her thoughts. "Here, Keisha, Tasha called you a couple of times." Keisha calls Tasha back. "Hey, girl, what is up?" "Kei, nothing, dude is feeling me, girl, he is talking something. The sad part about it is he is our enemy. He is telling me that he got some deep shit. He wants to wait to see if I am loyal. Girl, I laughed. He keeps talking in parables, talkin' 'bout he lost a few niggas tryin' to get big. Then he was like that ain't gonna stop his grin, 'cause he flipped the shit. Now he gonna say how he want a female to settle down with. He wants kids to continue his legacy. Things be real out here. Girl, I'm gonna get every fucking information there is to get. Memba, I told you," Tasha says. "Cuz, be careful; do not let him get on to you, and the one named Paul, watch him, 'cause he's snaky. There is a lot of things to be said about him. He knew what he was doing, girl, I'm the one to let you know we out here being private investigators and shit. Anyway, you good, cuz, just be extra careful so we can clamp down on them bitches the real proper way." Keisha hangs up the phone.

CHAPTER 10

THE PARTY

Saturday morning, October 15, Sheeba wakes the ladies up. "Party time! Good thing Tony came yesterday and cut the boys' hair." "Yeah, that's true, Ma," Keisha agrees. "Well, I'm going to get ready and drop the party supplies at the guesthouse. Also, the people need to set up the activities around the pavilion so it's safe for the kids to move around. Ma, the place is really nice. You will love the outcome. Adults could just sit in the pavilion and watch the children play and go to different stations. One pavilion will be used for the face-painting station." "Oh, sounds good, Kei. Call me when you want us to get ready." "All right, Ma, tell Stacy that her mom should come around three; the party starts at four." "Okay, no problem," she assures her. As Keisha walks out of the house, her phone rings. "Hello," Keisha answers. "Oh hey, what's up, Tony?" "Nothing, checking in on you on your busy day." "Oh, I'm all right. What are you doing?" she asks. "I'm at the shop." "Oh, so are you coming to the party?" "Yes, it starts at five, right?" "No, it starts at four. I told you that yesterday." "You know, you're right, but remember we discussed me arriving at five, because work and my customers' appointments." "Oh yes, you're right about that. So I will see you then." "Cool." Tony hangs up the phone. Keisha continues to drive, and her phone rings again. "Hello," she answers. "Jasmine, what's up, bae?" Keisha laughs. "Girl, I knew you would get there before me. I am like fifteen minutes away. Let the people in. Remember, we paid for the whole day...Yes, I know it's good. Do you have your outfit?...Okay, I'm on my way." Keisha hangs up the phone. The nerve of me; it's almost noon. Good thing the ladies know how to do makeup, hair, and, well, everything we need. Keisha laughs. This party is going to be like that, she says to herself as she parks. Man, fifteen minutes coming like nothing. Keisha smiles as she gets out of the vehicle. She walks into the guesthouse. "Man, every time I walk in here, I smile." "Keisha, this place is beautiful," Jasmine exclaims. "Yes, yes, that is why I wanted this place. Turning ten is a big deal," Keisha emphasizes. "True. Okay, so let us do our walk-through so we are sure where we want things to go. Look, you see right over there to your left is all wall space; that's where they should set up the picture booth. Directly across should be the candy table. The food should be right on the table in there; the kitchen area is gigantic. You know, we will need two tables together." "Jasmine, you on the roll with everything. All right, let's go outside. Food, picture booth, and candy table inside. Now outside in the large grass area past the pavilions, we will put the moon bounce. It's shaped like a basketball." "Oh, how cute, Keisha; I'm so proud of you making everything work out for Josh's birthday." "Jasmine, thanks, I told you it's a big deal. All right, so you have the moon bounce, face painting, and what else?" I purchased a basketball hoop so they can play 'how far can you shoot the ball.'" "Oh, interesting, so you have three stations." "Yes, that's good for them. Then we could play a game of balance the ball, and after that eat food, sing 'Happy Birthday,' and then end the party." "Sounds good, Keisha, sounds really good. Will someone like a special guest be coming?" "No, we have to lay low, so I did not think it was a good idea to hire a professional basketball player to come to his party." I feel like it would bring forth more crowd," Keisha answers. "Okay, that is reasonable. Better safe than sorry. Anyway, let's see what the people have to offer; they are setting up inside." Jasmine and Keisha walk back inside. "It's looking good in here. Josh is going to be surprised and excited." "Wait, hold up, we have to put the gift table in that back room right over there." Jasmine points to the back hall. "That's a great idea. We could have Ma collect his gifts and put them in the back room. Well, we have everything set. I wrote them a check." "Now we all can just wait," Jasmine says. "We could go and sit in the truck." The girls walk toward the front entrance. Keisha stops. "Excuse me, ma'am, how long is the setup?" "Oh, we will be done in another thirty minutes. It's a big place to fill," the lady says. Keisha and Jasmine continue walking. "Keisha, they are professionals; the place will look amazing when they're done, okay?" "Yeah, I guess you know." "Anyway, what's been going on with you?" "Jasmine, them dumb niggas are still watchin' the house. One day the neighbor saw them looking in the window." "Good thing you moved." "Shoot, who you tellin'. I'm grateful for that, but it's still on my head. You just never know these days. Another thing is Josh he keeps asking for Ang. Ma said surprise him, but after months will it be enough?" "Keisha, don't think too hard. You're doin' all that you're supposed to do." "True, but it's—" Jasmine cut her off. "Girl, it's nothing. Everything will fall into the right place." "True, I guess." "Keisha, it's nothing to guess." "Jasmine, these men need to stop trying to intimidate us. They need to go sit down somewhere else." Jasmine laughs. "They'll soon get what they are asking for." "You are right: they'll soon get what they are asking for. Today it is all about Josh." "You and Tony still talking?" Jasmine asks. "Yeah, we talk more now. I'm thinkin' about giving him a chance." "Really? That's real cute, girl; you ain't talked to nobody since Lamar." "There was no one to talk to, and my interest in men was not there anymore

59

especially if you can't do nothing for me, what is the point?"
"You right, boo. Let me go check if they're done." Jasmine goes
into the guesthouse. The people meet her as she walks to the
front entrance. "Great, thank you all for coming out. I'm sure
it's beautiful," Jasmine compliments. "Hey, one question: Did
you all decorate the gift table?" "Yes, ma'am, everything is done."
"Wow, thank you so much. We like your services and will be sure
to post reviews. You guys did an amazing job." Jasmine shakes
the woman's hand. "Have fun with your party." "Thanks!"
Jasmine waves at Keisha, who rolls down the window. "She's finished. Meet you at your place." "Damn, it's one thirty already."
"Yeah, we will be at the house in like twenty if you drive fast."
"True. All right, I'm out." The ladies drive to Keisha's house.
Time is against them, and they have to quickly get dressed as
soon as they enter the house. Keisha is upset, because she woke
up late, and it made everything push. As she pulls in front of her
house, she gets a phone call. "Hello...Oh, what's up, Kevin? Are
you coming later?...Yeah, his party is today...Yeah, stop by,
please. Imma send the address. Tell Ang to come...Yes, Kevin,
but remember, it's his birthday. She never misses his birthdays...
Great, I knew you were playing games with me. Angie never
misses his birthday. Give her the address...Okay, thanks. Love
you, bro, see you later." Keisha walks in the house with Jasmine
following behind her. "Hey, what is up everybody? Oh good,
everyone is almost ready," Keisha says with a smile. "Josh and
Ryan, are you happy?" "Yes, I'm happy," Josh says, full of joy.
"Aunt Keisha, you got my favorite jersey?" "Yes, I tried to do my
best." "So, are we all wearing black?" Stacy interrupts. "Stacy, you
know we all picked up the same jersey with multiple team logos.
Josh is the only one wearing a Lakers jersey that's real." The
ladies laugh. "All right, we're gonna get ready." Keisha and
Jasmine separate, with Jasmine going upstairs and Keisha downstairs. "Mama Sheeba, we have to load the car with the fruit and
veggie trays," Stacy comments. "Yeah, let's put our clothes on

first. The ride to the location is far." "That's right. Boys, put your clothes on," Stacy directs. "Mama Sheeba, you're practically ready to put your jersey on, and I will do your makeup." "Okay, come to my room. It ain't nothing to put on my shirt." Stacy waits a few minutes as Sheeba puts on her undershirt and then her black jersey. "Look how nice you are, Mama Sheeba," Stacy says, delighted. "You want me to put your hair in a bun?" "Yes, moving around I don't need my hair in my face." "Sounds good to me. You have all that hair anyway; it should be put in a cute bun." Sheeba smiles. "Thanks, Stacy. My son is lucky to have such a loving woman like you." "He knows it, too, Mama Sheeba. He always claims his gratefulness." "Stacy, I'm next." Jasmine walks in the room. "I will make sure the boys look good and come back." She walks out of the room and makes a sharp left turn. "Boys, y'all ready?" Jasmine knocks before she enters. "Yes, we're ready." "Put some oil in your head. Come mek me do it," Jasmine says. "You boys look good; now go show Mama Sheeba and Stacy." The boys run up the two steps into the room beside them. "Grandma, look," they call out. "Oh yes, boys, you look sharp. Go downstairs and sit on the futon. We will be ready soon." "All right, I'm done." Stacy puts the mirror in Sheeba's hand. "Well, I'm glitzing," Sheeba says with the brightest smile. "Yeah, good gyal, Mama Sheeba," Jasmine adds. "I'm going downstairs with the boys." Sheeba gets up. We all could go downstairs. Ain't no need of staying up here," Stacy adds. "Yeah, come mek we guh," Jasmine says aggressively. The ladies go downstairs, and Sheeba stays with the boys in the living room. Stacy says while walking down the steps to the basement, "Yo, Kei, you ready? It's two thirty. The people for the food and games are coming soon. We told them three." "Yes, is Jasmine ready?" Keisha asks, looking up. "Yep, she is." "Jas, take Ma, and y'all go so they can enter. Bring the cake, please." "Stacy's ready," Jasmine says with excitement. She also reminds Stacy, "Hey, you're supposed to do my makeup quick." "Sit down, we don't have long,"

61

Stacy says as she starts. "What color eye shadow?" "Give me purple." "Great, Mama Sheeba was blue. I'm doing orange. What color are you doing, Kei?" "Yellow." "All right, we each cover one of the symbols on the jersey." "Yes, I know, it works out well," Stacy says, excited. "Make sure to do the eyelashes." "Jas, you ain't gotta tell me that," Stacy says. "See, quick and cute. Only fifteen minutes and I'm done." "Oh yeah, look at the shimmer on my cheekbone." "Yes, it looks great," Keisha comments. "Okay, Jas, go; time is running out." Jasmine runs out. "Kei, Jasmine is the best; she drives fast and safe. Plus, you know she always has an eye for greatness." "That's true. She is my other half; we should have been sisters." Stacy smiles. "I'm glad we're family." "Hey, Stacy, you make up a face so well." "Growing up that's all I did for my sisters and cousins. Trust me, there's a lot of us." "Oh, I see, like me, now. It was just Ang and myself as females. We all know Ang was not into the girly stuff, although she likes the finer things in life." "Yeah, it's just practice and what you enjoy," Stacy comments. "Boys, y'all ready? Because we are almost done down here," Keisha shouts. "Kei, are you wearing the wig or what?" "No, I think I'll do a bun like Ma, but add this piece to it so it can have more body." "Yeah, and it could sit up high." "Yes, Stacy, you know what to do." The ladies laugh and continue talking. "Okay, I think we are ready." Stacy turns Keisha around in her spinning chair. "Thank you, Stacy, thank you. I look wonderful," Keisha says. "Come on, boys, let's go and party." The ladies and boys walk out of the house. "Keisha, it's good that we left by three twenty; we won't get there until four or even minutes after, because you know Saturday traffic." "Yeah, Jasmine being there with Ma is helpful. She can greet the guest as they enter. Plus, you know we have everything set up for the party." "Alesha called me. She asked if we could go out. I declined it, because now that I'm unable to trust her, what's the point?" "Stacy, you gotta keep it the same, because we don't know what these people are about. If you decide to walk away from her, things might change for the worse. They don't know we don't know, especially Paul sneaking ass. Come on, boys, we are here." "Aunt Keisha, this place looks good," Josh says as he walks to the door. Walking in the place, Josh has a surprised expression on his face. Tears fill his eyes. "Aunt Keisha, I love it so much! Oh, man." "This place is tight!" Ryan shouts, spinning around in the center of the room. "Boys, go outside and explore the activities." "Oh, Ryan, look way over there past the little houses. Look, there is a moon bounce." "Oh, crap, it's shaped like a basketball. Let's go." The boys run past the pavilion. "Beat you there!" Josh shouts. Ryan laughs. "Whatever. Let's go in the moon bounce!" The boys take their shoes off and enter the moon bounce. Jumping and jumping, Josh hears someone calling his name. "Oh look, it's Mark. All my friends are here, Ryan; let's go," Josh says, jumping out of the moon bounce. The kids begin to gather around Josh. "Happy birthday, Josh," they say. He smiles. Looking around, his friend Mark says, "Josh, there is a lot to do. You have face painting, a moon bounce, the hoop game—you even have another game over there." Mark points to all the balls to the far left. "Yeah, well, let's have fun!" The kids scatter all over the place and stand in line at each station. The ladies walk around, mingling with the crowd. The party is nice, and the kids are having fun. Josh is laughing and smiling when Keisha looks over at her nephew. She has a smile on her face, having forgotten about all the drama that is going on their lives. Kevin and Tony walk in at the same time. "Oh, look at who popped in," Stacy acknowledges. "Hey, Tony, Keisha is outside assisting the kids." "Oh, all right, thanks," Tony replies while heading outside. "Baby." Stacy kisses Kevin on the lips. "Let me go say 'what's up' to little sis. Hey, where's Ma at?" Kevin asks suspiciously. "She's in the back room putting her grandson's gifts up." "Oh, aight, Imma link Kei real quick." Stacy admires her man Kevin as he walks away. He's 5'5", with brown skin, a nice build, bold legs, and wavy hair. He walks outside to Keisha, who is sitting in one of the pavilions.

"Kevin!" Keisha shouts. "Kevin, I'm so happy to see you." She smiles and gives him a huge hug. "Bro, you made my day." "Uncle Kevin!" Josh runs up. "Uncle Kevin, is Mommy here?" "No, not yet, but she is coming; she told me she was coming." "Okay." Josh gives him a handshake. "Go have fun, nephew," Kevin says proudly. "Sis, you did out the party nice, on the real note." "Yeah, I tried. Anything for Josh, Kevin, you know." "Yes, sis, exactly like that." Tasha walks over. "Hey, cuzzo, wah ah gwaan. Long time, mon long time. Where everybody at?" "They say they are coming. Justin should be on his way too." "Oh, for real?" "Yeah, for real, he should be on his way." "Oh, the party's almost over. We're 'bout to eat and sing 'Happy Birthday.'" "For real? It's six though." "Yeah, I'm unsure if they will make it for anything else." "Tasha, shut up and give them a chance. You ever see Angie not come to any of Josh's functions?" "You're not lying about that." The adults talk, drink, dance, and enjoy the party. "Hello, everybody," Keisha speaks into the DJ's microphone. "We are now going to eat, and after eating we'll sing 'Happy Birthday' to Josh. My mother, Ms. Mayer, will be handing out thank you cards as a token of our appreciation to you all. We ask that you allow children to get their food first. The adults will eat; there is plenty of food to be served; enjoy yourselves. Once more, thank you for coming and celebrating Josh's birthday with us." Keisha hands the mic to the DJ and walks over to the table to help serve the food. Josh looks around to see if his mother has arrived yet. He notices people leaving the party, and his head is held down as his grandma fills his plate of all his favorite foods. "What in the heck is this?" Keisha says as she looks at the time. Forget it, how could I explain this to Josh? She looks over at Josh. Well, he looks unbothered. Keisha continues to serve food. Josh eats his food, looking around as his cousins talk to him about his party. "Josh, your party is one of the best; I ain't lying," his cousin Renee says. "Yeah, I guess. Thanks," Josh responds. Tasha announces cake time. All the kids run to the table. "Come on, Josh," Keisha calls. He walks slowly to the table, trying to smile. Everyone begins to sing 'Happy Birthday' to him. Josh smiles to take a picture with his family. He keeps looking around for his mother. That is it, she ain't coming. Josh walks from the cake table. He finds a corner and slumps down. He holds his head in his knees. People are already leaving, too—until they hear Ryan running over to Stacy. "Mommy, Josh is crying, he is crying." "What?" Kevin turns back. "Man, hold up." He walks over to Josh. "Hey, man, what is up?" Josh continues crying. "Oh, man, stop crying." Keisha walks over. "Josh, come here, baby, come here." "What's wrong?" Sheeba walks over. While crying, Josh catches his breath; he sits there continuing to cry, thinking, This is the worst day of my life, the worst. Kevin says, "Nephew you had a bangin' ass party Aunt Kei put together for you." Josh looks around, still crying. Keisha holds him, trying to comfort him. Josh continues to cry and scream, "This is the worst day of my life!" The adults begin to cry as they watch Josh break down in Keisha's arms. No one knows what he is crying for, except Keisha. Josh keeps crying and screaming, "This is the worst day of my life!"

- THE END -

www.ingramcontent.com/pod-product-compliance
Lightning Source LLC
Chambersburg PA
CBHW071236170626
46809CB00008BA/3089